The Foot-Stomping Adventures
–of–
Clementine Sweet

WRITTEN BY KITTY GRIFFIN AND KATHY COMBS
ILLUSTRATED BY MIKE WOHNOUTKA

CLARION BOOKS ★ NEW YORK

Cashew

Clementine

Chestnut

Cinnamon

Chili Pepper

Cupcake

Clarion Books
a Houghton Mifflin Company imprint
215 Park Avenue South, New York, NY 10003
Text copyright © 2004 by Kitty Griffin and Kathy Combs
Illustrations copyright © 2004 by Mike Wohnoutka
The illustrations were executed in acrylic on watercolor paper.
The text was set in 17-point Centaur.
All rights reserved.
For information about permission to reproduce selections from this book, write to Permissions,
Houghton Mifflin Company, 215 Park Avenue South, New York, NY 10003.
www.houghtonmifflinbooks.com
Printed in China

Library of Congress Cataloging-in-Publication Data
Griffin, Kitty.
The foot-stomping adventures of Clementine Sweet / written by Kitty Griffin
and Kathy Combs ; illustrated by Mike Wohnoutka.
p. cm.
Summary: When her family ignores her on her sixth birthday, Clementine gets mad and starts stomping on
people with her very strong legs and super tough feet, but a tangle with a tornado turns things around for her.
ISBN 0-618-24746-7 (hardcover)
[I. Behavior—Fiction. 2. Texas Hill Country (Tex.)—Fiction. 3. Humorous stories. 4. Tall tales.]
I. Combs, Kathy. II. Wohnoutka, Mike, ill. III. Title.
PZ7.G881358Fo 2004   [E]—dc21   2003004024

SCP I0 9 8 7 6 5 4 3 2 I

Custard

Cherry

Coconut

Caramel

*To Kim, who has danced through
this life by my side, and Mother,
a real sweet stepper in her day*
—K.C.

*To that fella on my dance card, Jerry,
and to my sweet-as-sugar sister, Doris*
—K.G.

To Caitlin, Conner, Kaitlin, and Simon
—M.W.

Cider

Cantaloupe

Chiffon

Crabapple

Folks in Lovett reckon their town to be just about the sweetest little town in the whole entire Texas Hill Country.

But it wasn't always so.

There was a time Lovett 'bout blew off the map.

4

They had a spring, but it dried up.
They had bluebonnets, but not enough for a bouquet.
They had a dance hall, but it was closed.
And they had *one little thing* folks tried real hard to steer clear of.
I bet you're itchin' to know what in tarnation that *one little thing* was . . .

Clementine Sweet—that's what. The meanest, most ornery and pugnacious, pigtail-wearing, pint-sized person in the whole entire Texas Hill Country.

Don't get me wrong. Clementine hadn't always been spiteful. When she was born (the youngest of fourteen), she had a smile as sweet as honeysuckle.

I suppose by now you're not only itchin', you're a-twitchin' to know what could turn a little gal from sugar to vinegar . . .

Being forgot about—that's what.

Two days before Clementine's sixth birthday, the Sweet family reunion started. Sweets rolled in from everywhere to have a romping, stomping, good ol' Sweet time.

The Tennessee Sweets challenged the Texas Sweets to a hoedown. There was so much stompin' and hollerin' and spinnin' that the barn began to clatter and clank till it seemed likely to fall apart. But no one paid any mind. They just kept a-dancing. All night, all day, they carried on . . . right past Clementine's birthday. No one wanted to be the first to tucker out.

The only one who noticed her birthday missing was little Clementine. She sat as patient as a peanut on the edge of the dance floor, wearing the birthday hat she'd made herself, just a-wonderin' who'd be the first to wish her a happy birthday.

That's when cousin Snickerdoodle slid by and said, "Hey, Caramel, what's with the dumb hat?"

Clementine stomped her foot. "I'm not Caramel. I'm *Clementine.*"

Then cousin Strudel scooted past and hollered, "You look silly in that ol' hat, Cashew!"

Clementine stomped both her feet. She shouted, "Cashew's a boy. I'm *Clementine,* and don't you forget it!"

Then her brother Chestnut came by. "Is that a new dance? The stomp?" He laughed and got so mixed up about who she was that he went through all the Sweet names he could think of but never did come up with calling her Clementine.

That did it. The cork popped. Clementine clenched her fists. Her face heated up, and her smile turned upside down. She marched over to Chestnut and shouted, "I'm **CLEMENTINE SWEET!** I'm gonna stomp your feet!"

With a quick one-two, she did just that. Then she hollered, "And don't you forget me ever again!"

Soon the Sweets began to take notice of Clementine.

"What's that girl doing running over the hills like that?" Papa Sweet asked. "You'd think a hive o' hornets was after her."

"She's making her feet extra tough and her legs extra strong," complained Clementine's brother Chili Pepper. He pointed to the bandage on his toe. "I forgot to save her some hot sauce for her tacos."

And even though Clem's parents put her in time-out every afternoon, it didn't slow her foot stomping. By the end of summer, the doctor suggested that the whole entire Sweet family wear steel-toed shoes. He told Mrs. Sweet, "I've never seen such strong legs or such tough feet."

Mama Sweet nodded. "Yep, she's been outrunning the roadrunners."

When Clementine started first grade, the teacher, Miss Mud Pie, didn't call on her even though her hand shot up higher and she bounced harder than all the other kids in the class. Finally, she popped right out of her seat, stomped Miss Mud Pie's toes, and ran home. Clementine spent the next three days sitting in a room for kids who misbehave. When she returned to her classroom, Miss Mud Pie was wearing a pair of high-heeled steel-toed shoes.

'Fore long, Clem didn't even wait for folks to forget about her before she stomped them. She started stomping on strangers' feet too, just to be sure they noticed her. Soon everybody tried to stay out of her way. When folks saw her walking down one side of the street, they crossed over to the other.

After a spell, the people of the town began realizin' that visitors to Lovett were getting scarce as sweet dog's breath.

Ben Birdbath said, "I'm plumb worried. I might have to shut down the café."

"The spring's dried up, the few bluebonnets we got ain't blue, and there's no place to dance," No-Neck Norman grumbled.

"What few folks do come have to be steered clear of that Clementine Sweet," Granny Gurney said.

"If'n something don't change, this little town's liable to dry up and blow away," Norman added.

Norman didn't realize it, but change was on its way.

The very next day, Cinnamon said, "Clementine, Mama and Papa are going to the Fire Ant Festival, so you're coming to the Bluebonnet Café with me today."

Clementine grumbled as she put on the apron Cinnamon handed her.

"Smile," Cinnamon said. "Customers don't like frowns." She put her hands on her hips. "And absolutely no foot stomping!"

"Okay," Clementine promised.

She meant to keep her promise. Really she did.

About the time Clementine and Cinnamon arrived at the Bluebonnet Café, so did a right peculiar, walloping, wicked wind.

Thunder rumbled through Lovett like a herd of runaway longhorns. Lightning crackled like sparks from Clementine's boots.

Just then a big ol' bus rolled into town and pulled up beside the café. A large band piled out and tumbled inside.

"Why, it's that Kyle fella," Granny Gurney said.

Kyle nodded politely and took off his hat. "I sure could use something to drink," he said.

The bass player hollered to Clementine, "Hey, honey, can we get some iced tea?"

Clementine twirled around faster than a cracking whip.

The town folks froze stiffer than starch. They knew what was a-comin'.

Yep, Clementine tromped up to him and shouted, "I'm *Clementine Sweet*. I'm gonna stomp your feet!" And with a quick one-two, she did just that. "And don't you forget me."

Then the drummer said, "Why, don't get so fired up, sugar."

Clementine spun around faster than No-Neck Norman's fishing reel.

The town folks froze stiller than sticks. They knew what was a-comin'.

Sure 'nough, Clementine shouted, "I'm **Clementine Sweet**. I'm gonna stomp your feet!" And with a quick one-two, she did just that. "And don't you forget me."

Kyle stood up. "What on earth put that frown on your face and made you so mean, pumpkin?"

Clementine shouted, "Don't call me 'pumpkin'! You heard my name. I'm **CLEMENTINE SWEET**. I'm gonna *STOMP* your feet!" But when she went to do just that, Kyle took two quick steps back. Clementine took two steps forward. He stepped two steps left. She stepped two steps right.

Then Kyle called out, "Hit it, boys."

The band members grabbed their instruments and started playing.

Kyle stepped up. Clementine stepped back. Kyle stepped side. Clementine stepped side. Folks could see sweat on Clementine's brow. Her frown began to turn upside down. He stepped. She stepped. He stepped. She stepped. They stepped so fast that Granny Gurney had to fan herself to keep from fainting.

Just as the salt shakers shimmied right off the table, Ben Birdbath burst in from the kitchen shouting, "TWISTER!"

The band stopped playing. Clementine and Kyle stopped stepping. Everyone ran to the window. Sure enough, on the horizon was a funnel cloud.

"It's headed this way!" Granny Gurney yelled.

"But there's not room in the storm cellar for all of us," Ben Birdbath shouted.

"Oh, no!" cried the band.

"Don't you worry," Clementine hollered. "I'll fix it!" She dashed out of the Bluebonnet Café running so fast that she kicked up a cloud of dust the length of the Guadalupe River. When she got up to the twister, she saw that it was spinning from west to east. So she ran around it from east to west. Faster and faster she ran on those very strong legs and those super tough feet. Faster and faster.

"She's untwisting the twister!" No-Neck Norman yelled.

"She's our darling Clementine," Granny Gurney said.

"No," Kyle said. "She's your *daring* Clementine."

Clementine eyeballed a small piece of the tornado that was hanging in the air. She stomped her feet. It still hung there. She double-stomped her feet so hard that the earth cracked open and a new spring sprung up. She stomped once more, and that last bit of twister broke into pieces and headed toward the heavens.

A tired-out Clementine staggered back to the Bluebonnet Café.
She pulled off her boots and wiggled her toes. "I'm Clementine Sweet,"
she said. "Want to smell my smokin' feet?"

Well, I suppose by now you're triple itchin' like a flea sitting in a fire
ant's nest to know how this little story turned out . . .

"Let's put up a statue to thank Clementine!" yelled Ben Birdbath.

"I don't need a statue," Clem said. "Just open up the dance hall and
let me dance."

So the people got together and reopened the dance hall. They named
it the Sweet Times Dance Hall in honor of Clementine. And they hung
up a sign that reads, HOME OF DARING CLEMENTINE SWEET, THE BEST
SWEET STEPPER EVER.

The next Sweet family reunion was held in the hall. Everybody
danced for days, shaking the walls and rattling the floor, but the only
person who danced past Clementine's birthday was Clementine herself.
She two-stepped through the hall, blowing out all seven candles on all
seven cakes while the town folks sang "Happy Birthday!"

Now, folks in Lovett say their town is the sweetest little town in the whole entire Texas Hill Country, especially 'cause of *one little thing*—Clementine Sweet. Everyone knows Daring Clementine Sweet stomped the ground so hard that a spring sprung up that never runs dry. On that same day, blue must have fallen from the heavens because now the bluebonnets around Lovett are the bluest bluebonnets anywhere. Buses come from all over so tourists can see them. Kyle and his band even parked their bus and stayed a spell.

Today, the whole entire Sweet family helps run the dance hall while Clementine teaches folks to dance. Visitors stay over on Saturday nights to hear Kyle's band at the Sweet Times—and to see the smile on Clementine's face as she slides across the dance floor on her sweet two-stepping feet.